Owl AND Eleanor
Meet the New Kid

Book 3

Written by H. M. Bouwman • Illustrated by Charlie Alder

For Alannah! Welcome to the family!
And with much thanks to Naima Abdi for
so much good discussion and helpful information.
Many blessings to you, Naima.

First edition published 2019
Printed in the United States of America
25 24 23 22 21 20 19   1 2 3 4 5 6 7 8

Paperback ISBN: 9781506452029
Ebook ISBN: 9781506452036

Illustrations by Charlie Alder
Cover design by Alisha Lofgren, 1517 Media
Interior design by Eileen Engebretson, 1517 Media

Library of Congress Control Number: 2019932335

V63474;9781506452029;MAR2019

Beaming Books
510 Marquette Avenue
Minneapolis, MN 55402
beamingbooks.com

Chapter 1
Eleanor

Eleanor was having a boring *boring* Friday afternoon. When she came home from school, there was no one to play with. Her best friend Owen, who lived in the duplex apartment above hers, was not home. He'd left a note on the door that said, "We are at the Science Museum. We will be home soon." But what did *soon* mean? Did soon mean in five minutes? Or did soon mean in five years? Owen once said that Galapagos tortoises lived for a hundred years or even longer. Five years wasn't soon to Eleanor, but maybe it was really fast if you were a Galapagos tortoise.

Owen wasn't a tortoise, so maybe soon really did mean five minutes.

Eleanor waited outside Owen's door for five minutes. Owen did not come home.

When she went downstairs to her family's apartment, her dad was cleaning the kitchen. He didn't like cleaning the kitchen, but he did it to be nice to the family. Eleanor decided to be nice too. So she and her kitten helped sweep the floor until her dad told her that they had helped enough and maybe they should do something else. Then she practiced doing cartwheels in the living room until her dad said cartwheels were only for outside. Then she went in the backyard.

But the backyard wasn't that much fun without Owen. Even Michael, Owen's little brother, would be more fun than nobody. Why wasn't there anyone to play with? If there was another kid in the neighborhood, that might be nice. Even though Owen was her best friend, maybe another friend would be good too—one who played whatever games Eleanor wanted.

Just then, a truck drove down the alley—a pickup truck, with a sofa in the back held down by straps. The sofa did not have any sofa cushions, but it did have a brown-and-orange flowered design all over it. Eleanor watched it pass, but she didn't watch in time to see who was driving.

The truck pulled into the yard two houses over—the backyard of the house that had a *For Rent* sign in front.  Eleanor checked to make sure no one else was coming, and then she ran down the alley and peered around the fence.

The truck was parked behind the For Rent house. Maybe there was a new kid who would follow all her directions and play all her games whenever Owen wasn't around!

The truck door opened. A man got out, a small thin man with dark skin, darker than Eleanor's. He had gray hair mixed in with the black. *Gray hair*. And he moved like he was tired and sore. Or very old.

The other truck door opened, and a teenage boy got out. Eleanor slumped. Teenagers were no good. They didn't play with you, and they definitely didn't follow your directions.

The teenage boy reached into the cab, pulled out sofa cushions, and stacked them on the back of the truck, while the old man unlocked the back door of the house. They looked like they were moving in. A teenager and an old man. No one the right age. Eleanor sighed and walked down the alley.

She climbed the stairs to Owen's apartment. At least she could tell Owen about the new neighbors, even though they weren't anything interesting. But the Science Museum note was still on Owen's door, and Owen *still* wasn't home. Did he even know what *soon* meant? Eleanor grabbed a marker from downstairs and crossed out the word soon on the note and wrote "IN A MILLION YEARS." She wrote really big and put four exclamation marks after it (!!!!) to make sure that Owen would realize how late he was.

Then she went down to her own apartment and found Goldfish the kitten. But Goldfish didn't want to play and instead stalked away to sleep somewhere that wasn't near Eleanor.

Eleanor flopped on her bed in the room she shared with her older sister Alicia. Alicia's pillow was gone, and her backpack wasn't at her desk either. Dad poked his head into the room and said, "Alicia is at Millie's for a sleepover. Remember, honey? And I'm going to grade papers for a little while, so don't bother me unless it's an emergency."

Ugh. It was such a boring afternoon that Eleanor even missed Alicia.

After a while, the front door opened, and a scratchy, kind-of-deep voice said, "Dad, I'm starving! Is there any food?"

It was Eleanor's brother Aaron. He was in high school. He was tall and skinny and had brown hair like their mom instead of almost-black hair like their dad and Alicia and Eleanor.

And he was way better to talk to than no one.

Eleanor ran to the kitchen. The dishes were all clean and there were apples in the bowl on the counter. Aaron picked one up and bit into it. "Did you see that the house down the street has been rented?" he said. "I wonder who's moving in."

"Old man and a teenager," said Eleanor. "No one interesting. They have a boring flowered sofa."

Aaron laughed. "You're like a super-detective, coming up with all that information on the new neighbors."

It sounded almost like Aaron was making fun of her. "I could be a super-detective. If I wanted to," said Eleanor.

"I'm sure you could."

"I'd figure out all kinds of stuff about the new people."

Aaron dropped his apple core in the little compost bin. "Want to come out and help me rake? Dad wants us to get the backyard done today."

"Dad wants *you* to get the backyard done today."

"You can jump in the leaf pile when we're done making it."

"Will you call me Darth Vader? Or—what's a detective name?"

"Sherlock Holmes."

"Sherlock. That's what you have to call me. Sherlock Vader."

"Deal. But you have to actually rake."

They dug the rakes out of the entryway closet that their family shared with Owen's family and went to the backyard. There were a lot of leaves on the ground, and they were all different colors—red and yellow and purple, along with some sad, crumpled brown leaves that were starting to melt into the ground. Eleanor and Aaron only needed to rake the grassy part of the yard, not the way-back part near the alley, the part Eleanor called the forest because of all the trees there. That part was covered with pine needles and leaves, and they left everything there to turn into dirt. The grassy part, though, needed clearing, and it was big enough that Eleanor was a little tired just looking at all the leaves.

Aaron started raking right away. "Let's get going, Sherlock Vader," he said. "Big leaf pile, remember?"

Eleanor raked one rake's worth of leaves, and it formed into a teeny tiny pile that a mouse could maybe jump in. It would take

about a million rakings to make a big enough pile for her. "I'm going to deduce something," she said. "Like a detective. I deduce that there are a million leaves on this lawn."

"I think that's more like a guess," said Aaron.

"Not if I count them."

"Well, okay. Or you could count how many are in one rakeful, and then count how many rakefuls you do, and then add them all up."

That sounded like way too much counting. "I have a different theory. I think . . . that the new neighbors are old old people."

"With a teenager?"

"He was probably their grandson. He was helping them move in."

"Okay. Well, it would be pretty easy to solve that puzzle—you could just ask them. Keep raking, please."

Asking wouldn't be any fun. "What if you couldn't ask, though? Then how would you figure it out? What would a detective do?"

"Well, I guess you'd observe and draw conclusions from observation," said Aaron. "Like . . . you'd watch what furniture they brought into the house, or who seemed to be there when they moved in. Or you'd look at their mail to see who it's addressed to." He paused. "*Don't* look at their mail. That's illegal."

No mail. That was fine. Eleanor started raking super fast. She had just thought of something she and Owen could do that would be interesting. They could be detectives, and they could spy on the new neighbors. Eleanor and Owen both still had a lot of space left in their journals from when they wrote essays about their lives. They could use the notebooks for detective notes, and they could collect clues—

"This went much faster than I thought it would," said Aaron. "We've got a big leaf pile. Want to jump in it?"

She looked up at the house and saw a light flicker on in Owen's second-floor apartment. "Maybe later. I gotta go. Owen and I have some work to do."

Chapter 2
Owen

Meanwhile, Owen and his little brother Michael and their dad had had a good time at the Science Museum. Owen read all the description signs in the dinosaur-bones room, which he wanted to do; Michael pushed all the buttons on the talking descriptions, which he wanted to do; and they both climbed on the "PLEASE CLIMB ON ME" pretend-dinosaur exhibit just outside the dinosaur room, which both of them wanted to do. And later, in the exhibit on electricity, all three of them—Dad included—made their floppy hair stand straight in all directions.

After they rode the bus back to their own neighborhood, they walked the last block home. And as they neared the For Rent house, Owen's dad paused. "The sign is gone."

Sure enough, the For Rent sign was not there.

"It's not the For Rent house anymore," said Michael sadly. "Hey, can I run all the way home?"

"Yes," said their dad. Home was only three houses farther. Michael raced away.

Owen stopped to look at the For Rent house. It almost looked lonely without the sign in the yard. "Do you think someone rented it?"

"Probably," said Dad. "And, maybe it's someone with kids. More kids on the block would be nice, right?"

More kids? Did they really need more kids than him and Eleanor? Owen felt a little lurch in his stomach. What if the new kid was really cool, and Eleanor liked the new kid more than she liked Owen?

Then he shook his head to himself. No. She had just said the other day at the ice-cream store what good friends they were, and that she liked Owen exactly the way he was. She would stay his friend even if a new kid moved in. He knew that.

But the question was still there. Did they really *need* a new kid in the neighborhood? Weren't Owen and Eleanor happy the way things were? Why should more kids move in?

"What are you thinking, sweetie?" asked Dad.

"Just thoughts," said Owen. "Nothing important."

Michael was already on the steps of their duplex, panting. They were home.

Almost as soon as they got inside the apartment, Eleanor was at their door, knocking very loud and fast. Owen let her in, and she blew past him into his and Michael's room. "Michael," she said, "there is a giant leaf pile in the backyard."

Michael yelled to his dad and ran outside.

"Let's go," said Owen, starting to the door. A leaf pile sounded good.

But Eleanor didn't run downstairs right away. She stood in the middle of Owen and Michael's room. "There are new people in the For Rent house."

"I know," said Owen. "We saw."

"You saw the new people?" She sounded disappointed.

"No, we saw that the For Rent sign was gone."

"Oh, good. I think we should be detectives. I even have detective glasses and a detective coat for us and everything. And we have spy notebooks."

Owen was confused. What did this have to do with the new people in the For Rent house?

"We'll spy on the new people and observe them, like detectives, and figure out who they are and what they are like."

"That's kind of like the scientific method," said Owen. "We just talked about this at the Science Museum today. Did you know that scientists observe things and make theories?

We were talking about dinosaurs—"

"I did not know that," said Eleanor, bouncing on her toes. She bounced when she was excited. "We're not going to be scientists. We're going to be detectives. But if you want to be a scientific detective, that's fine. We'll find out all about the new people."

"We will?"

"Yes. And we'll keep detective notes in our notebooks. I'll wear the spy glasses since you have your own glasses already. But you can wear the detective coat if you want."

Owen thought about it. Detective sounded like a good game. And he was curious about the new people. "Okay. Can we jump in the leaf pile now?"

Eleanor stopped bouncing and froze, a shocked look on her face. "Yikes! We better hurry, or Michael will get all the good jumps!"

First they grabbed Owen's notebook from his room and stopped at Eleanor's apartment to grab her notebook too—and the spy glasses and detective coat. Then they ran outside.

Michael was half-hidden under the pile of leaves, only his lower body sticking out, legs kicking.

"What are you playing?" Eleanor called to him. "Wait, I'll detect it." She shoved the glasses onto her face. They wobbled on her nose and rolled their googly eyes. Spy glasses didn't normally have googly eyes, Owen was pretty sure, but these were Aaron's Mad Scientist glasses from Halloween a long time ago. Eleanor said they were just like real spy glasses.

Owen rolled up the sleeves of the white detective coat (also from Aaron's Mad Scientist costume) so he could use his hands. The pocket of the coat, which held his notebook perfectly, said "Dr. Frankenstein" on it in official-looking black letters. Eleanor said he'd be Frankenstein the Detective and she'd be Sherlock Vader.

Eleanor tried to explain all this to Michael, but he didn't seem interested. He was still head-first in the leaves. "I'm busy. I'm digging a hole to catch a fairy." Michael's legs slowly disappeared into the leaves.

"Well, we need a turn too," said Eleanor. "I raked that pile."

"By yourself?" asked Owen, impressed.

"Aaron helped."

Michael emerged out of the side of the pile, covered with leaves. "The fairy escaped," he said. He wandered off to the woods at the back of the yard.

Eleanor took off her spy glasses and Owen took off his real glasses so they wouldn't get smooshed, and they put their glasses on the little table near the house. Then they held hands and ran together as fast as they could toward the pile, Eleanor yelling, "Charge! Defeat the Empire!" and Owen imagining that all of the *Star Wars* Empire soldiers were standing against them and they were detectives, racing into unimaginable danger. They didn't need any more friends. They needed exactly what they had now.

Owen and Eleanor jumped, and leaves went flying, and everything was perfect just the way it was.

Chapter 3
Eleanor

That afternoon, Eleanor helped Dad with supper until her helping got too loud, and then she was sent to the living room to color quietly until Mom came home from work. She colored loudly, but no one seemed to notice, not even Goldfish the cat, who stayed asleep on the sofa next to her.

When Mom came home, she first said hi to Dad, who came out of the kitchen. They called each other sweetheart and other mushy things in Spanish. Dad called Mom a little duck and gave her a kiss.

"You know I can understand you," said Eleanor. "And, weird."

"We aren't trying to be sneaky," said Eleanor's dad. "If we were, we wouldn't talk at all in front of you."

"When we met, we met speaking Spanish," said Eleanor's mom. "So that still feels right for talking to each other sometimes." They had met in Costa Rica, where Eleanor's dad was living because that's where he was born and grew up, and where Eleanor's mom had moved for a job. That was all long before Eleanor was alive, of course.

Dad called Aaron, and they sat down for supper.

After they prayed and started eating, Eleanor said, "We have new neighbors, but my theory is that they are old and boring."

"Theory?" said Mom.

"I think she's pretending to be a detective," Aaron said.

"Owen and I are the most famous detectives in the universe," said Eleanor. "I even have spy glasses."

"Binoculars?" asked Mom.

"What are those?" Eleanor said.

Dad went to the closet and got out an old pair of binoculars. If you put them to your face, everything far away got really big. It

 was actually very hard to see anything through them, but they made you look very detective-like. Eleanor asked to borrow them.

"That's fine," said Dad. "But no spying through people's windows."

As if she would.

(But she had been thinking about it.)

Well, she would just spy on things in the street and peek into the moving truck when it got here.

As they ate, everyone had things to say about their day—what they learned in school, what they ate for lunch, what the walk to the bus was like, all of it. Finally, long after Eleanor was done eating and had started to get wiggly, supper was over.

"My detecting skills say that we are having ice cream for dessert," said Eleanor.

"Hmm," said Dad. "Really?"

Eleanor ran to the freezer and opened the door. There was no ice cream inside.

"Well, that's one way to find out," said Mom. "You could also ask your parents."

"Are we having ice cream for dessert?"

"No."

As they cleared the table and Mom started washing dishes, Dad said, "Here's a question: Does Eleanor know her spelling words for Monday? How would I find that out if I were a detective?"

Eleanor shook her head slowly. *Uuuuugh.*

"I'd give her a quiz," said Aaron, grinning. "Come on, Ellie, I'll run through the list with you. You can prove you know your words."

Eleanor proved she knew some of her words—eight out of ten. (She was pretty sure she would never, ever understand how spelling worked—if *who* and *what* and *when* and *where* and *why* all started with *WH*, then why didn't *how*? *Whow* did spelling even make sense? On top of all that, *would* just wasn't a fair word at all. Sneaky little *L*.)

After the practice quiz with Aaron, Eleanor ran upstairs to see if Owen was done with supper.

Owen and Michael and their dad were still

eating, Owen at a normal speed and Michael very slowly. They were about to have dessert, so Owen's dad phoned downstairs to see if it was okay for Eleanor to have some too. And since she hadn't had dessert at their own supper, she got to have it with Owen.

IT WAS ICE CREAM.

Eleanor gasped when she saw the little bowls. "I'm an amazing detective!" Of course, then she had to explain what she had detected about their freezer, all the way from downstairs. She felt super smart. Exactly like a world-famous spy. Maybe she should put the googly eyes back on.

"We were just talking about the new people before you got here," said Owen. He took a bite of ice cream and chocolate syrup.

"I knew that!" she said. "Because of my detective skills. What did you say about them?" She took a giant bite, and the syrup dripped a little bit on her chin.

Usually Michael, who was five, was even messier than Eleanor, but today he was only taking tiny bites, smaller than Owen's. He said, "The For Rent house isn't for rent anymore."

"My dad met them this afternoon," said Owen.

They all looked at Owen's dad, who was drinking milky coffee and not eating ice cream. Owen's dad smiled and put his cup down. "I didn't *meet* them; I just saw them for a second when I went for a run this afternoon. They were pulling into the alley with a few pieces of furniture. We waved at each other. When I stopped by to say hi on my way back from my run, they were already gone."

"Was it a flowered sofa?" said Eleanor. "In a pickup truck?"

"Nope. A kitchen table and some chairs," Owen's dad said.

"How many chairs?" said Eleanor.

Owen's dad frowned like he was trying to remember. "Maybe five?"

"They waved," said Owen. "That seems friendly."

"Did they have toys? Bikes?"

Owen's dad shook his head. "Not that I saw. But I'd guess they're moving in for real this weekend, so we'll find out soon."

"Well," said Eleanor, "my detective skills tell me that they are old people who sit on a flowered sofa all day. But we need to detect more to be sure. It's also possible, since they have five chairs, that they are a mom and dad with triplets who are the same age as me and Owen, and the triplets know how to shoot targets with a bow and arrow and they also know how to build tree houses, and they'll build a tree house in their backyard and then they'll shoot an arrow over to *our* tree house—because we'll build a tree house in our backyard, too—and the arrow has a string attached to it, and then we catch our end of the string and the triplets hold onto their end of the string, and we tie the string between the two tree houses, and then we have a high-wire act between the two tree houses and we all learn to do tricks on the high wire, and when the circus comes to town, the circus owner asks us all to star in their show."

Owen's dad said, "That's a very long, very specific theory."

"I'm a detective," said Eleanor. "It's my job to find out if it's true or not." She lifted her bowl and tipped it to get the last drips of melted ice cream into her mouth.

Owen ate his last spoonful and nodded.

"We could wait for them to move in this weekend and then ask them if they have triplets . . ."

Michael's spoon clattered into his bowl, which wasn't even empty. His cheeks were red. "I'm not hungry. Can I eat my ice cream later? Can you save it for me in the fridge so it doesn't get melty?" He sounded tired.

"Oh," said Owen's dad. "Of course." He put the ice cream in the freezer, and by the time he came back, Michael had gone into the room he shared with Owen and crawled into his bottom bunk bed. Their dad went to take Michael's temperature.

"I deduce," said Eleanor, "that your brother is sick."

Chapter 4
Owen

Michael was still sick on Saturday morning, so Owen was supposed to be quiet—which was fine, since he and Eleanor wanted to play outside anyway. Or, as Eleanor said, they wanted to be detectives out in the wild.

"I think this is actually a lab coat," said Owen. They were standing in the backyard. Eleanor was squinting around the googly eyes in her spy glasses, and Owen was rolling up his sleeves again on the Dr. Frankenstein jacket. "Like scientists use."

"But scientists aren't as cool as detectives," said Eleanor.

Really, Owen thought scientists sounded pretty cool too.

Eleanor twirled around and fell over into the tiny remains of the leaf pile, which was now really just crumbs mixed into the brown grass. (Aaron had bagged most of the leaves last

night with Owen's dad after supper.) She sat up and pushed the googly eyed glasses back up her nose. Owen wasn't sure how she could see anything around the googly eyes. "These glasses aren't working very well."

"I wear glasses all the time," said Owen. "Real glasses. They don't make you a detective. I mean, you can be a detective without them too."

Eleanor studied him, ducking her head and squinting around the googly eyes. Then she took off the fake glasses and put them in her pocket.

guess it's better to be a spy who can see."

Owen sat down next to her on the leaf crumbs. "What's our plan? Do we watch the new people?"

Eleanor said, "We'll sneak down the alley when we hear the truck come, and we'll watch them unload. But what can we do until then?" She jumped up like she wanted to spy *right now*.

Owen said, "We have our notebooks. Maybe we should write down all our clues so far."

Eleanor started turning wobbly cartwheels across the lawn. "The family is super old. That's my first clue."

"I'm not sure that's a clue," Owen said. But he wrote it down. "Why do you think they're old?"

"Flowered sofa. Only old people buy flowered sofas."

"But *we* have a flowered sofa. We got it from our grandma."

"Okay . . ." said Eleanor, thinking between cartwheels. "Then another theory is that they have a grandma who gave them a flowered sofa."

"Or they could have bought it at the thrift store." That was where Owen and Michael's dresser and bunk bed came from. "Or maybe they *like* flowers on sofas."

Eleanor wrinkled her nose as if that option didn't make sense at all. "Now watch!" She ran across the lawn and did a flying side kick. Run-run-run-run-jump-KICK-land-fall. Then she ran back and did it again the other direction. Run-run-run-run-jump-KICK-land-fall.

Owen thought some more. Then he wrote down "CLUE" in the notebook. Under "CLUE" he wrote "flowered sofa." And next to that he wrote a list of all the things that a flowered sofa could mean. "My dad also saw five chairs and a table."

"Which means parents and triplets." Eleanor ran back and forth across the lawn. It made Owen feel a tiny bit tired to watch her, but he knew she liked to run and jump while she talked. Running and jumping helped Eleanor think.

Owen wrote down "table and five chairs" on the CLUE side of the page, and then wrote "triplets" next to it, and also wrote down two more possible explanations: "five people in the family (not triplets)" and "extra chairs for visitors."

"And we know about the old man and the teenager," said Eleanor, "because I saw them in the truck."

Owen wrote down the old man and the teenager as a clue, and then he added two theories: "Teenager is just helping" and "Teenager lives here." Then he paused because he had a big question.

"Do we . . . ? Eleanor . . . ?" He couldn't think of a good way to say what he wanted to say. And maybe it wasn't a detective question. But it was important.

Eleanor finished her kick and her fall and her getting up, and then she skipped back to Owen. "Do we what?"

Owen put the notebook down and looked up at her. The sun made a bright halo behind her head, so he couldn't see her face very well. He needed to ask his question, even if it sounded weird or bad. Even if he felt kind of mean saying it—because it didn't sound very friendly to him. "I know this isn't a clue and it doesn't belong in the notebook. But I don't exactly know how I *feel*. I mean, our block is really nice the way it is. Do we *want* there to be kids in this family? Like, a new kid who is our age? Do we want more kids in the neighborhood? Or do we not?"

Chapter 5
Eleanor

Eleanor was surprised by Owen's question. She had never thought about whether they *wanted* a new kid in the neighborhood. She had just been excited to find out all about the people moving in and to try out her spy skills. And now that Owen asked the question, she realized that maybe they *didn't* want a new kid their age. *Did* they? She wasn't sure. Things were good just the way they were, like Owen said.

On the other hand, a new kid might be really good at playing with her when Owen wasn't around. A new kid might follow all her directions—which not even Owen did.

On the *other* other hand, a new kid might not want to play the same games that she and Owen liked. A new kid might not even know who Sherlock Vader was, and a new kid might not want to play laser-sword fighting or superheroes or spy. A new kid might be really *different* from them.

She decided to put her googly-eyed glasses on to think about the problem, but the glasses had fallen out of her pocket sometime during all the cartwheels. They glinted at her from the grass. She ran over, picked them up, and jammed them on her nose.

The glasses did not help. She didn't feel smarter.

"So, do we want a new kid?" Owen asked again.

Eleanor said, "I don't know."

Eleanor's mom called her back inside because Eleanor hadn't made her bed or picked up her room, which, according to her mom, she was supposed to do every Saturday—actually, she was supposed to do it every *day*, according to her martial arts teacher. She usually did something in between what her mom wanted and what her martial arts teacher wanted. But today she'd been too excited about being a detective, and she'd forgotten to do any picking up at all. Her room was kind of a mess.

Owen had already picked up his room last night before bed, because that was his family rule, so he helped Eleanor shove her toys into the closet while she made her bed and put her art supplies away. Alicia was finally back from her sleepover, and she was lying on top of her bed with her eyes closed like she was tired. "Try to be quiet," she said. "I only got three hours of sleep last night."

"It was a *sleepover*," said Eleanor. Did Alicia not understand the word?

"We were up talking really late," Alicia

said, yawning. "And watching a movie. And we did our fingernails."

Eleanor picked up Alicia's limp hand and studied it. Her nails were super pale pink and sparkly. Usually Eleanor loved pink sparkly things. But if you could paint your  nails any color in the universe, why *wouldn't* you make them look like bloody claws of death? She didn't understand Alicia at all.

Owen's face looked like he didn't think pale pink was the right color either. With her spy skills, Eleanor just knew he must be thinking of bloody claws of death too.

But what if there was a new kid in their neighborhood who didn't understand about bloody claws of death? What if the new kid thought super pale pink was the right color for fingernails?

Eleanor shuddered. "Let's go back outside and wait for the big truck. We need to figure out who exactly is moving into our neighborhood."

They hid under the big pine tree in their front yard. The pine tree was on the corner of the yard nearest to the For Rent house, and it had huge drooping branches that came down around them like a tent. Owen and Eleanor could both stand up under the tree if they stood near the trunk. And they could sit on the pine-needle-covered dirt that, if you used your imagination, felt just like a soft carpet. The branches were thick with needles. If someone stood outside the tree and stared at it, that person would only see the very bottom of them sitting on the dirt—and even then, only if the

person was looking right at them and knew they were there. Owen and Eleanor tested out the hiding spot before they got under the tree, making sure it was really hidden. It was a good spot for making scientific observations. The new people would never think to look under a tree while they were moving in.

They sat under the tree for ten whole minutes before the moving truck showed up. Owen had an old watch of his dad's in his pocket, so they knew how long they were sitting there.

Ten minutes was a long time.

Ten minutes was long enough to build a mountain out of pine needles, make little pinecone people march up the mountain on a journey, and have a horrible storm blow them down the other side of the mountain. It was long enough to build a tiny cabin out of twigs for more pinecone people. It was long enough for one of you (Eleanor) to run back inside for Dad's binoculars and bring them out. It was long enough to realize that when you're hiding under a pine tree, you can't really see much with binoculars and mostly you are looking at pine needles. It is long enough to pull a magnifying glass out of your pants pocket (Owen) and study pine needles, and it is long enough to realize that pine needles under a magnifying glass look exactly the same as regular pine needles, just bigger. It is long enough to play hangman two times on

Owen's notebook paper—and long enough for each person to win one time. And it is long enough to start getting bored.

Finally, after ten minutes passed and Eleanor was just about ready to say she was done being a detective, something happened.

The big moving truck arrived.

And the old man and the teenager got out of it.

And then something else happened.

A car arrived, right behind the big truck.

And a woman and girl got out of it.

A girl about their size. A new kid.

Chapter 6
Owen

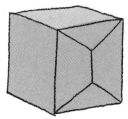The first thing Owen noticed about the new kid was that she was wearing a scarf on her head that covered up all her hair and a long skirt that went all the way to the ground. The second thing he noticed was that her skin was brown, darker than Eleanor's.

Or maybe he noticed her scarf and her skin color the other way around—things were happening so fast, he couldn't tell.

He also noticed that she wasn't smiling. She stood with her arms wrapped around herself like she was cold. Or maybe unhappy?

The woman (the mom?) was wearing a scarf over her hair too, and a long skirt just like the girl. The teenage boy and the old man (who did not look *that* old to Owen, not like a grandpa age, anyway) did not wear scarves or hats on their heads. They had brown skin like the woman and the girl, and they had short, very dark curly hair—except where the man's hair was gray.

Eleanor whispered, "Four people. One of them is a kid." She raised the binoculars to her face, focusing for a few seconds before wrinkling her nose and dropping them. The binoculars clunked against her chest on their string while she peered through the branches with her bare eyes.

Owen nodded, then realized Eleanor couldn't hear a nod. "Yeah. A kid who looks like she is our age."

The man took a key out of his pocket and unlocked the door, and the four new people went inside. The door shut. They were inside the For Rent house.

Owen and Eleanor stayed hiding under the tree, just in case the new people came out. They sat on the pine needles, and Owen took out his notebook and wrote down their clues and observations. "Make it sound detective-y," said Eleanor.

Owen thought maybe she wanted to write it down herself, but when he held the notebook out to her, Eleanor shook her head. She was scooping needles into a pile.

So Owen wrote down the people's hair and their clothes and their head scarves. He showed Eleanor the clues.

"Why are they dressed so weird?" asked Eleanor.

"It's probably not weird to them," said Owen. "My dad said that Muslim people sometimes wear a scarf over their hair. The girls do, I mean, and the grown-up women. So maybe they're Muslim." He wrote it down.

"Do you think the woman is the mom of the girl?" Eleanor asked.

Owen wrote it down. "And maybe the grown-up man is the dad?"

"He has gray hair!" said Eleanor. "*Some* gray hair," she corrected herself. "Anyway, I think gray is more of a grandpa thing."

"Maybe he's an old dad," said Owen. "Or maybe that's just his hair color. Like yours is black and mine is yellow-brown."

"Mine is brown," said Eleanor. "Super-dark brown." She pulled some out from her head and crossed her eyes looking at it. "Yep, dark brown."

Owen wrote down the theories about the man ("Maybe a dad with gray hairs?" And "Maybe a grandpa?") and the theory about the woman ("Maybe a mom?"). Then he wrote down "THE KID: looks like a girl. Maybe Muslim. Maybe just like wearing things on her hair. Maybe covering her hair because unpacking is a dusty job." Then he was out of ideas.

"That's a good one," said Eleanor, looking over his shoulder as he wrote. "My mom used to wear a scarf on her head when she cleaned the garage at our old house. What's *Muslim*?"

"It's a religion," said Owen.

"What kind of religion?"

"I'm not sure exactly." Owen felt kind of bad, like he should know. He had asked his dad one day, at the grocery store, why a group of ladies had scarves on their heads even though it wasn't cold out, and his dad had said,

"Maybe they're Muslim—that's a religion," and Owen had been about to ask what that meant, but then Michael had fallen out of the grocery cart, which he was trying to crawl into even though Dad said not to, and when he fell, his arm hit some soup cans, which slid off the shelf and rolled down the aisle, and Owen and Dad had never gotten back to their discussion.

"Look!" Eleanor whispered loudly, jabbing Owen with her elbow and pointing through the branches. Then they both shushed, because the people were coming back out of the house, smiling and talking.

They went toward the big truck and opened the back. The woman laughed and said something, and the girl replied. The girl was facing toward Owen and Eleanor even though she was talking to her mom, so Owen and Eleanor could hear her really well.

She was speaking a different language.

It was definitely not English. And it was not Spanish either. Owen knew that because he had already learned a little bit of Spanish in homeschool. Eleanor knew a ton of Spanish from having a dad who talked Spanish, and Owen could tell from her face that she didn't recognize this new girl's language either. Eleanor elbowed Owen again, and he nodded.

The girl went to the truck and climbed inside the back as the man and teenage boy started unloading furniture. Eleanor muttered under her breath, naming the items as they unloaded them and brought them into the house: "Small table, another chair." Like she was trying to memorize clues.

The girl handed down an armload of clothes on hangers to the mom, who carried

them in. Then the girl wheeled a bike down the ramp, a bike that looked too big for her. Then she wheeled down another bike that looked like her size. She parked them next to the truck, looking up and down the street like she was checking to make sure there were no bike thieves. The teenage boy came out from the house and said something in the foreign language, and the girl wheeled the bikes onto the porch while he unloaded a dresser with the older man.

More and more stuff came off the truck. Under her breath, Eleanor was naming and counting it all: "One bookcase, three mattresses, two rugs, one more dresser."

The new girl called something out to the

teenager, who said something back to her. Owen wished he could tell what they were saying. The language was pretty, with rolling r's and long vowels in places he didn't expect them.

"She doesn't speak English," said Eleanor.

"We don't know that," said Owen.

"She's talking in that other language!" said Eleanor.

"But to her dad and her brother. Sometimes you talk in Spanish to your dad, but you still know English."

Eleanor was scrunching up her face now to listen. Owen did the same. Maybe if they listened hard enough, the new people would say something they could understand.

Then the big brother walked to the truck and said something that must have been funny, because the girl laughed and made a fist and pumped her arm.

"I know what *that* means," murmured Owen.

"It probably means something totally different in their country," said Eleanor.

"What country?"

"I don't know. Wherever they are from."

The new kid ran up to the truck, and the teenager handed down a bag that was half as big as she was. She dragged it to the sidewalk and bent over it.

"What is that?" said Owen. He moved a branch aside to see.

"Probably something from her country," said Eleanor.

The girl pulled a red thing out of the bag and tossed the bag back to her brother. It was hard to see what the red thing was through the pine branches, but it was flat. And it had little wheels . . .

It was a skateboard.

The girl stepped onto the skateboard and zoomed off down the sidewalk, waving to her brother. She was really good at skateboarding.

She skateboarded all the way to the corner and back, then back toward Owen and Eleanor and past their pine tree and to the other corner and back. Like she owned the whole block. Like she belonged there.

Chapter 7
Eleanor

Hidden in the pine tree with Owen, Eleanor watched the girl with the skateboard roll up and down the sidewalk. The girl skated fast, down to the near corner and back. She skated slow, looking at each house as she passed it. She rolled medium-fast right past the pine tree Eleanor and Owen were hiding in—and she didn't even look in their direction. She weaved and she went in a straight line and she weaved again, all the way down to the far corner.

"I deduce that she's not allowed to cross the street by herself," said Eleanor, when the new girl turned around at the far corner and started skateboarding back toward them. "I bet she's not allowed to go around the block by herself either."

"Shhh," said Owen as the new kid got nearer.

The new girl was humming. Owen could hear the music as she got  closer again. He didn't recognize the tune, but the girl had a nice voice. She held her arms out for balance.

Owen sneezed.

The new girl hopped off her skateboard and looked all around. Owen and Eleanor shuffled back, hiding behind the trunk of the tree as much as they could. For a minute it looked like the girl was staring right at them.

Then she got on her skateboard and rolled away, her back straight and her skirt flapping in the breeze.

"That was close," whispered Eleanor.

Just as the new kid got to the corner, Alicia yelled for Eleanor to come in to lunch. Anxiously, Eleanor and Owen watched the new girl to see if they could sneak out without her noticing.

The new girl kept going—around the corner.

"She gets to go around the block by herself," said Eleanor. "No fair!" Owen and Eleanor weren't allowed to go very many places ever since their running-away incident last summer. They definitely weren't allowed to go around the block by themselves.

Then Owen's dad called Owen from the upstairs window. "Lunchtime!"

Owen and Eleanor both peeked out to make sure no one from the new family could see them, but there was no one in sight. The rest of the family must be unpacking things inside. So they ducked out from the tree and ran toward their own house.

When they got inside, they both paused on the bottom landing before going into their own apartments. "Did you see her skateboarding?" asked Eleanor.

"Of course," said Owen. "She was good, wasn't she?"

"And did you see her biking?"

Owen looked confused. "She didn't ride the bikes. Neither of them."

"Exactly," said Eleanor. The new kid not riding a bike was important. It was weird. "*We* ride bikes."

Owen didn't seem to be listening very much. "What language was she talking?"

"Exactly," said Eleanor. "*Exactly.*" What language *was* she talking? Something that they didn't know. Something different.

Owen nodded, but he looked confused. "Exactly . . . what?"

From inside, Alicia yelled, "FOOOOOOD. WE ARE ALL WAITING!" She was yelling at Eleanor in Spanish and rolling the r of *esperando* in a very impatient way. Then she yelled, even louder, "TORTUGA!" and she rolled the r again.

"That's *turtle*!" said Owen in surprise. "I just learned this word in Spanish homework! She's calling you a turtle!"

"I'M STARVING!" yelled Alicia, now in English.

Eleanor ran inside her apartment, and Owen ran upstairs to his.

After they prayed, which Eleanor barely listened to because she was too busy being mad at Alicia, Eleanor said, "I think calling someone a turtle is name-calling."

"Not if you're actually as slow as a turtle," said Alicia.

"No fighting," said Eleanor's mom.

Aaron ate his sandwich in big bites. He worked as a bagger at the grocery store down the street, and he had to go to work right after lunch.

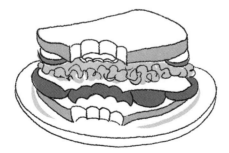

Dad said, "It looks like the new neighbors are moving in."

Eleanor nodded. "And they dress funny and talk a funny language."

"Eleanor," said Dad. He said her name in that voice he used when he was disappointed.

"What?"

Dad said, "Maybe I talk a funny language too, to some people. *Verdad*?"

"You talk Spanish—and English. Those aren't funny. They're normal."

Alicia rolled her eyes. "Also, maybe you dress funny."

Eleanor wore glittery things. Glittery things weren't funny. They were cool. "Maybe your *face* dresses funny," said Eleanor.

"Enough," said Mom. "Really."

Dad said, "I think I'll see if our new neighbors want any help with unloading. Anyone want to go over there with me?"

Aaron shrugged. "I gotta get to work, sorry. Oh, I'll bring some milk home."

Mom said, "Alicia and I are going to volunteer at the rummage sale, remember?" It was like a big garage sale, but in the church basement instead of in a garage.

"Eleanor? *Corazoncito?*" said Dad. "Want to see if you and I can help the new neighbors?"

Eleanor swallowed her sandwich bite, which tasted dry and made her cough. She took a gulp of milk. "Nope, sorry. Owen and me are busy."

"Owen and I," said Dad.

"Owen and I. Are too busy." It was true, kind of. They were busy collecting clues about the new people. Besides, did she really want to help them move in? Did this neighborhood really *need* or *want* a new kid—a weird new kid with a different language and different clothes—to move in? Owen's question was getting bigger and bigger in her head. A kid who was so different-looking from Eleanor and Owen would definitely want to do lots of things differently. What would happen to Eleanor and Owen's cool games? The new kid might wreck everything.

"Well, if you change your mind, you can always come over and help," said Dad. "And then you can welcome the new people into the neighborhood."

Eleanor took a giant bite of her sandwich, nodding like she agreed. But did she *want* to welcome the new kid?

Chapter 8
Owen

Owen and his dad had lunch by themselves, because Michael was sleeping and Mom was still at work. She was a paramedic, so she always worked for a whole night and day and then she didn't work for a couple of days. This was her night and day to work.

Dad made peanut butter and jelly sandwiches and carrot sticks and apple slices. He was a writer. If he made sandwiches, that meant his writing was going well. If he made a fancy meal, that meant his writing was not going well and you should not ask about it.

Dad prayed before they started eating. He thanked God for good food. He asked God to help Michael feel better and help Mom have a good day at work. He asked God to take care of the new neighbors and welcome them to the neighborhood.

When he finished, Owen said, "Did you meet the new neighbors for real yet?"

"Not yet," said Dad. "Eleanor's dad is going to head over there this afternoon to see if they need help unloading, but I'm staying inside with the sick kiddo." He paused. "Maybe I'll make cookies."

Owen said, "I don't know if they eat cookies."

"No?"

"They're . . . they're different from us."

Dad set his sandwich down to listen.

"The girl and the mom are wearing scarves on their heads and long dresses. Like the ladies at the grocery store that one time."

"Hmm." Dad picked up his sandwich again and took a bite, thinking. "Well, you might be right."

"That they're different?"

"That they don't eat cookies. There might be special foods they eat or don't eat. It sounds like they might be Muslim. Some Muslims have certain foods they don't eat."

"Like Peter." Peter went to their church. "He doesn't eat peanut butter."

"Because he's allergic. This is a little different, because it has to do with religious beliefs. But yeah, I wouldn't make peanut butter cookies for Peter. And I don't want to make foods for Muslims that they can't eat."

They ate a little more in silence. Dad was staring at the wall and chewing. When Dad was in the middle of writing a book, he daydreamed a lot. Owen liked that, because then Owen could daydream at the same time.

For his daydream, he thought about the new girl. Did she eat peanut butter? What kinds of things didn't she eat? When did she learn to skateboard? Could she do jumps and tricks? Did she also ride a bike? Would she want to bike down the sidewalk with Owen and Eleanor? Or maybe she'd want to walk to the park with them and one of their parents and bike up and down the cracked-up basketball courts that no one used during the day? Could she do a wheelie? Would her skirt get caught in the spokes? Did she talk English? How would they understand each other if she didn't?

And did he and Eleanor really want someone new in the neighborhood? Someone they maybe couldn't understand?

Dad must have been still daydreaming about food because after a while he said, "Well, we have a lot of grapes and some apples and bananas. I'll dig that little white basket out of the closet and bring over some fruit.  That should probably be okay." He pulled out his phone and tapped into it. "Yeah, it looks like that would probably be okay if they're Muslim. And bread too, maybe. I'll make some rolls while Michael's sleeping."

"Is he feeling better?"

"Yep, he has a cold and a little fever. I think he'll be fine by tomorrow." Dad stretched. "Want to walk the food over with me when the bread is done? Meet the new folks?"

Did he want to meet the new kid? Today?

And without knowing exactly what she was like first? Maybe he and Eleanor should do more detecting first. Then they would know if they wanted to be friends with her. "Um, Eleanor and I have some plans. But maybe later."

"I'll let you know before I head over there. Don't you two leave the yard without permission." That was because of last summer.

Owen nodded. "We'll stay in the yard." They would, for sure. They'd be under the tree, watching the new girl.

Dad looked like he might start picking up dishes, but Owen suddenly wanted to sit for a few more minutes. He wasn't quite ready to go outside yet. And he wasn't done with his sandwich. "Will you read more *Charlotte's Web*?" That was the book he and Michael and Dad were reading together right now.

Dad shook his head. "Not without Michael."

"Will you reread the last chapter? I really liked it."

Dad smiled. He liked rereading. Sometimes he reread a whole book for himself just for fun. "Sure." He got out the book and read aloud while Owen slowly finished his sandwich. It was the chapter where Wilbur the pig meets Charlotte the spider. Dad read even when Owen was done with his sandwich and got out his coloring pages from last week's Sunday school. The coloring pages were pictures of people doing nice things for other people, and the verse at the bottom said to love your neighbor.

The verse never said exactly who your neighbor was, though. Was it anyone who moved in next door, no matter who they were?

Charlotte the spider and Wilbur the pig were neighbors in the barn, and now they were starting to be really good friends. They were completely different from each other, too. Charlotte actually ate other bugs. For a living. And Wilbur was a pig who didn't know how to spell. And they were still friends. Owen wondered if they would stay friends through the whole book.

While Owen was thinking all these thoughts, he colored so hard his crayon broke.

When Owen finally ran downstairs to find Eleanor, she was running upstairs to find him.

They peeked out the front window to make sure no one was outside on the sidewalk. Then they raced out to the tree. The girl was still on her skateboard—or maybe she was on her skateboard again. Maybe she'd had lunch too, while they were eating. Anyway, she was on her skateboard rolling toward them from far down the street, almost to the corner. She was wearing jeans now, it looked like.

Owen almost thought the new girl saw them; she stuttered on the skateboard and just about fell over, and then she fixed herself and rolled even faster. She was going the fastest ever when she passed the pine tree this time, and her head was way up in the air.

She really looked like she knew what she was doing.

Eleanor muttered, "She doesn't even have a helmet on. She could hurt herself." But she didn't sound worried. She sounded like she wished she could ride a skateboard too.

The new girl was wearing a long sweater over her jeans. The sweater was purple and had glittery buttons and glittery designs on the front. She still had her scarf covering her hair, and now Owen could see that it had some glittery threads in it too.

"She has my shoes!" said Eleanor.

For a second, Owen thought Eleanor meant that the new girl had stolen her shoes. "How . . . ?" he asked. But then he looked at

Eleanor's feet and saw she was still wearing her shoes. They were white sneakers (now kind of gray from all the dirt and pine needles) with pink trim and bright pink shoelaces. The shoelaces were so bright that they almost hurt Owen's eyes.

He studied the new girl as she turned and came back toward them, now slower but weaving in a fancy pattern over the sidewalk. Yes, she had the same shoes. He just hadn't noticed them when she was wearing a long skirt.

Then, suddenly, her white-and-pink shoes tipped the skateboard up, and her feet jumped onto the sidewalk, and the skateboard stopped moving forward and so did the shoes. Right in front of their tree. And then the new kid said something. In English. And she sounded kind of angry.

"Hey. Why are you hiding in a tree? And why are you watching me?"

Chapter 9
Eleanor

When she asked why they were hiding and watching her, the new kid did not sound super happy. And Eleanor didn't know what to say. It suddenly seemed like telling the new kid that they were detectives who were spying on her might not be . . . exactly nice. She hid the binoculars behind the tree trunk.

Owen was crawling out from under the pine tree. He had to crouch down to squeeze under the branches. "Hi," he said.

"I'm Owen. And this is Eleanor."

Eleanor was still beneath the tree. Did she want to come out? It was so . . . she didn't know the word she wanted, but it was so *something* to crawl out from under a tree after you'd been caught spying. So embarrassing? Maybe that was it.

Owen said, "Eleanor?" He peeked under the tree.

The new kid peeked under the tree too. And Eleanor was just standing there.

"I'm not hiding," she said. "I'm exploring. Like a detective might explore things."

"You were spying on me," said the new kid.

"Want to see our fort?" said Eleanor. "Under the tree?"

The new kid shrugged. "Sure." She tucked her skateboard under her arm and ducked under the branches.

They all three sat on the pine needles.

"Nice skateboard," said Owen.

"Nice shoes," said Eleanor.

"Thanks," said the new kid.

Then there was a long quiet time. But it didn't feel boring-but-comfortable like Owen's daydreaming, which Eleanor was kind of used to. It was much, much worse.

She didn't know what to say.

Eleanor *never* didn't know what to say! She felt like her head might explode with all the different ideas floating around in it.

Finally the new kid said, "Well, I'm going to go." She started to crawl out.

Owen said, "Wait!" He looked at Eleanor like he wanted her to say something, but Eleanor couldn't. She just couldn't. Nothing would come out.

"What?" said the new girl. Kind of impatiently.

"I'm Owen," said Owen.

"I know," said the new girl. "You already said that."

"And this is Eleanor."

"You said that too."

"We live in this house with the pine tree. Eleanor's family lives on the bottom floor, and my family lives on the top floor. You're the new neighbor." He said it like it was a little bit of a question.

She nodded.

"What's your name?"

"Ifta."

"Ifta?" Owen said it slowly.

"I never heard that name before," said Eleanor.

"Well, it's a very normal name. Lots of kids have it," said the new girl. "I never heard of your names before I moved here."

"To this house?"

"To America."

"Where are you from?" asked Owen.

The new girl shrugged. "We flew here from Kenya. But my family is really from Ethiopia."

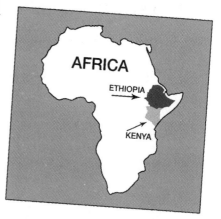

"Those are both countries in Africa," Owen said to Eleanor. He'd been learning lots of maps for his homeschooling. Eleanor's class hadn't gotten to Africa yet. They were still studying George Washington, and now she thought maybe they should study Ethiopia too.

"We're going to study Ethiopia in school," she said. "After George Washington."

"That's nice," said Ifta.

"What school do you go to?" asked Eleanor.

Ifta explained that she was going to start at Eleanor's school on Monday, after they were all done moving in. "We lived way across town when we first got here, and I went to a different school, but now we're moving closer to some of my cousins, and so . . ." She shrugged. "New school. But I'll still go to the same mosque, where lots of my friends are."

"Mosque?" said Eleanor.

"It's like a church, I think," said Owen. "For Muslims. Is that right?" he asked Ifta.

"Kind of," said Ifta. "I go to madrasa there on Saturday and Sunday mornings, and I study Arabic, and I learn lots of things about God and how to live a good life. I have a lot of friends there." She shrugged. "But I had some good friends at my old school too."

There was kind of a long quiet time again.

Then Owen said, "I'm sure you'll make lots of friends at Eleanor's school. Right, Eleanor?"

"Right," said Eleanor. Owen was trying to tell her something, but she wasn't sure what it was. School was awesome. Of course Ifta would make new friends. Kids played on the swings at recess, and sometimes they did a parachute game in gym class, and they made messy art with lots of glue, and during quiet time they read books. Eleanor was in the middle of a book about a Japanese American girl named Jasmine who liked to make mochi, which sounded like a really cool food.

Suddenly a question popped into Eleanor's head. "Do you eat mochi?"

"What?" said Ifta.

"Never mind," said Eleanor. "What is Kenya like?"

Ifta looked like she was thinking hard about what to say. "It's very different from here," she said, finally. "I lived in a refugee camp there."

"Is that where you learned to skateboard?"

Ifta laughed. "No, I didn't have a skateboard there. My cousin gave me his old skateboard when I moved here."

"Is the teenage boy your cousin?" asked Owen.

"What games did you play in Kenya?" asked Eleanor at the same moment.

"Yes, he's my cousin. In Kenya we played soccer sometimes." She paused. "It was just a lot different from here."

"And you're Muslim?" asked Eleanor. "And is that why you wear a scarf on your head? And that's a religion, right? And what language do you talk, besides English?"

Ifta stared at her. She looked the way Eleanor felt sometimes when her mom or dad asked her a lot of questions about school on a day that she'd gotten in a little bit of trouble for being too loud. She looked like she was tired of answering questions. "I can speak four languages," she said slowly. "English is my third-best."

"Wow!" said Eleanor. That was impressive. "I only know two. And Owen knows only one and part of another one."

Owen nodded.

Ifta said, "I learned Oromo from my family—that was our language in Ethiopia. And I learned Swahili at the camp, and a little bit of Sudanese there too. And English when we moved to America. Mostly my parents and I speak Oromo to each other."

Owen said, "Can you . . ." He trailed off.

"Teach us Oromo?" said Eleanor.

Owen shook his head. "That would be fun, but that's not what I was going to say." He looked at Ifta like he really wanted to ask for something and he wasn't sure if it would be polite. Eleanor could tell. And then, suddenly, she realized what it was Owen wanted to ask.

"Can we try your skateboard?" she said. "And can you teach us how to do it?"

Ifta grinned and stood up carefully so that she didn't smash her head against the branches. "Sure. Let's go."

Chapter 10
Owen

Owen ran to get his bike helmet, and Eleanor's too, and he convinced Eleanor to wear it because he said she was so brave she'd probably crash and she didn't want a damaged brain, did she? He lent Michael's helmet to Ifta. Michael had a really big head for his age, and the helmet fit Ifta just fine.

"Now we can *really* go fast," said Eleanor.

But they couldn't. It turned out that skateboarding was harder than it looked, and it was hard just to go in a straight line down the sidewalk. But Ifta was a good teacher, and she laughed at herself almost as much as she laughed at Owen and Eleanor.

Eleanor's dad was helping Ifta's parents and cousin unload the truck. He waved at them as they took turns riding on the skateboard. When it was Ifta's turn, she rode to the corner and back, easy-peasy. When it was Owen's turn, Eleanor held one of his hands and Ifta held the other, and they helped him stay up while he slowly wobbled. When it was Eleanor's turn, she said she didn't need help, pushed off very fast, jumped onto the skateboard, yelled very loudly, and crashed very quickly. She did really good falls that she had learned in martial arts class, though, and she landed in the grass, so she was okay.

All in all, skateboarding was wonderful.

After Owen's dad brought fruit and bread over to the new neighbors, Ifta had to go inside to unpack her clothes and help her mom clean and move things around. So Owen and Eleanor went inside their own duplex, after agreeing to meet on the sidewalk again after supper if they were allowed to, for more skateboarding.

In Owen's apartment, Michael was awake and sitting on the floor with his building set. He was building a monster. He had a very runny nose.

Dad said he would read more *Charlotte's Web* if Eleanor wanted to hear it too, and Eleanor did. Owen told her what the story was about so far, and they both got crayons and paper to draw.

While Dad read, Owen didn't draw Wilbur the pig or Charlotte the spider. Instead, he drew a girl in a long dress and a scarf, riding on a skateboard. He drew the way Ifta looked when he first saw her and didn't know her

yet, with her skirt whipping in the breeze as she rode past the pine tree. She had a little smile on her face because she was skateboarding so well. Then, because Dad was reading about Charlotte, Owen drew a spider on the branch of the tree and a web that had the word "Brilliant!" woven into it.

Eleanor drew a giant purple spider with a million little round eyes and ten legs. The legs were purple too. The spider was wearing ten little white-and-pink sneakers.

Dad finished the chapter.

"I like Charlotte," said Michael without looking up from his building set.

"She's a good friend," said Dad.

"Even though she eats bugs," said Owen. He couldn't imagine eating bugs.

"I'm not sick anymore," said Michael. He swiped at his nose with his sleeve.

"Dad," said Owen, "I have a question. It's not about the book. It's about friends who are really, really different from each other."

"Like me and Owen," said Eleanor.

"Even more different," said Owen. "Like, they know different languages and they come from different places, and they have different religions and different ways they think about God, and they are just really, really different."

Dad tilted his head and closed the book. "What is your question?"

"Can they still be friends? Does it matter that they are so different?"

"It doesn't matter at all!" said Eleanor. "Because they can skateboard and they can talk in English, probably, or even in sign language if they have to, and they can play after church and madd—I forget the name."

"Do you mean madrasa?" said Owen's dad. "Where kids go to learn about Islam?"

"Yeah, that. Those kids are really not different at all."

Owen looked at his dad. He wasn't sure Eleanor was completely right. He wasn't sure it was okay to pretend there were no differences, because it seemed like there *were* differences. But he also wanted to be friends. And not just because you were supposed to love your neighbor. Also because Ifta was cool and fun.

"Differences make a difference," said Michael solemnly. "Charlotte is my friend. She's different. I like her that way."

"Charlotte isn't your friend," said Eleanor. "She's in a book. She's Wilbur's spider friend."

"There's a different Charlotte in the corner of our bedroom. And she's my friend," said Michael. "That Charlotte doesn't even go to church. She goes to madrasa. We talk about it all the time."

"You talk to the spider?" said Dad.

"There's a spider in our bedroom?" said Owen.

"This is about Ifta," said Eleanor. "And she is so interesting! I want to get to know her more and more, and then someday I want to learn to speak Oromo, and then we can talk to each other in Oromo. Or maybe we will both learn Korean, like my martial arts teacher. That would be cool too. Oh! And, Owen, she has to meet our kitten! And we need to learn more skateboarding from her."

Owen's dad smiled. "That all sounds like fun."

Owen looked at his drawing, with Ifta and the spider. Eleanor always thought of the fun things about meeting new people. He wanted to think about the fun things too. But he also knew that he and Ifta would be different in lots of ways. And the differences were good things to talk about and learn about. But for being neighbors—for being friends—what mattered was loving each other.

Chapter 11
Eleanor and Own

After reading time, both kids had some things they needed to do. Eleanor needed a bath. Owen needed to help sweep the floors of their apartment. Then there was supper. After supper, they went back outside. Ifta wasn't there. But when they knocked on her door, her mom answered and smiled and called for her.

Ifta said, "I can only play a little while. I have to take a bath."

"Me too!" said Eleanor. "I mean, I already did. But it's totally okay if I get dirty again."

They took turns on the skateboard, and then they leaned the skateboard against the steps of Ifta's porch and sat down to rest. Ifta said the house was nice  inside, much bigger than their last apartment. Her uncle and aunt might come to live with them soon, so it was good that it was big.

"Do you have your own room?" said Eleanor. "Owen and I have to share rooms—me with my sister and him with his brother. I used to have my own room." Ugh. Sharing with Alicia was hard.

"It's hard to sleep all by myself," said Ifta. "It's very quiet."

"Was it different in Kenya?" said Owen. "At the camp?"

Ifta nodded. Then she said, "Are there other Ethiopian kids in your school? Or Muslim kids?"

"I'm not sure," said Eleanor. "In my class, anyway, there isn't anyone who wears . . ." She pointed to Ifta's scarf, not sure what to call it.

"A hijab?"

"Yes," said Eleanor. "So maybe you'll be the only kid at our school who is Muslim *and* rides a skateboard *and* speaks four languages. You'll be very cool."

"I'm still learning English," said Ifta. "I don't write very well yet. English has tricky spelling."

"That's right!" said Eleanor, glad to have something important they could agree on. Spelling was horrible. "But really, don't worry about your English. My dad has been in America forever and he's super old and he's *still* learning English. You can hardly tell, except when he doesn't know the word for something hard, like a bug's name or something. Owen and me can help you with hard words just like we help my dad."

"Four languages is amazing," said Owen.

"So did you live in Kenya a long time?" said Eleanor. "My grandparents live in Costa Rica, and I might visit there someday. But Owen and I have never lived anywhere interesting."

Ifta said, "I was born in Ethiopia, but I don't remember it because we moved to Kenya right away. I only remember the refugee camp." She shifted, and the wheels on the skateboard whirled next to her. "I like it here a lot. It's safe here. And maybe we can . . . ride bikes together someday? I really like riding bikes."

"We love riding bikes," said Owen.

"This is awesome!" said Eleanor.

They sat on the steps and talked until the moon came out and the stars showed and the night breeze turned so chilly that they were all shivering, even in their sweaters and sweatshirts. They talked until Owen's mom arrived from the bus stop on her way home from work. Owen's mom met Ifta and then told Owen and Eleanor that they both had to come inside in five minutes so that they'd get to bed on time and be able to go to their churches tomorrow.

When their five minutes were almost up, Ifta's mom poked her head out of their front door and said Ifta needed to get to bed so she

could go to madrasa at their mosque the next morning.

They all sat for just one minute more, looking at the stars, before they had to go in.

Owen sighed, not because he was sad but because he was happy, and also because he had just figured out something important, and that felt like a thing to sigh about.

"What?" said Eleanor.

"What?" said Ifta.

"Nothing," said Owen. "I'm just glad we all moved here. And I'm glad we're all so different. There is so much for us to talk about and learn about. And I'm glad we're all friends."

"Me too," said Eleanor.

"And me," said Ifta.

About the author:

In addition to the Owen and Eleanor stories, **H. M. Bouwman** writes historical fantasy for older kids, including *A Crack in the Sea* and *A Tear in the Ocean*. She is a professor at the University of St. Thomas and a mom of two homeschooled kids.

About the illustrator:

Charlie Alder has illustrated many books for children, including her first authored and illustrated picture book, *Daredevil Duck*. She describes herself as "a curly haired coffee drinker and crayon collector." She lives in Devon, England, with her husband and son.

Other books in the Owen and Eleanor series

Owen and Eleanor Move In

When eight-year-old Eleanor moves into the bottom half of a duplex with her family, she is not happy. Her old home was way better. In her old home, she even had her own bedroom. Not any more—now she has to share with her big sister. The situation needs to change, and she knows just how to fix it. When Owen, age seven, meets Eleanor, he's excited—finally, someone to play with who isn't his little brother! He teaches her how to fence and write in code, and she helps him build mechanical gadgets and thinks his homeschooling is cool.

But when Eleanor asks Owen to help her escape back to her old house, he's not sure he should do it. . . . What should a friend do?

Owen and Eleanor Make Things Up

Owen is doing the same creative writing project for homeschooling that Eleanor is doing in public school! They have to write an interesting story about their lives. The problem is: their lives aren't that interesting. So Eleanor decides to fix the problem by doing exciting things—with not-so-great results. When they join a community martial arts class, Owen sees a different way to make an interesting story happen . . . by making something up that sounds true even though it isn't. When they both end up in trouble—again—they learn that making up fake stories to fool people isn't a good way to live.